My Quiet Ship

Hallee Adelman

pictures by Sonia Sánchez

Albert Whitman & Company
Chicago, Illinois

Whenever I hear the yelling,
I run to the spot.

Quickly I become commander of the Quiet Ship,
which takes me far, far away.
From here...from there...

from the sounds
that hurt my ears
and make my heart ache.

"Crew! I need you!" I call.
I gather them up one by one.

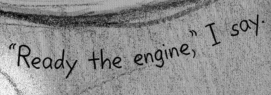

"Ready the engine," I say.

Then I grab spaceflight supplies.
We climb aboard the dark ship.

I turn on the light.
  "Time for the countdown."
  We whisper,
    "5...4...3...2...1...blast off!"

BRUM! BRUM!

The rumbling is so loud
that we can't hear anything else.

Then,
WHOOOOOSHHHHHH!

We travel
through the
clouds
and the stars

and the universe.

Far, far away
From here...
From there...
From that yelling.

Sometimes we get off the ship and explore other planets
with their smiling creatures
who hug us and speak in nice voices.

Sometimes we stay for a little.
Sometimes we stay for days.

But one night,
the yelling gets so loud
it breaks the Quiet Ship.
We can't take off.

We sit there trying to
draw happy pictures
   to forget about
   the sounds that make
my stomach sick.

The sounds that make me
want to shrink small
so that no one can see me
or remember that I'm nearby.

I start crying.
My pilot says, "What are you doing?
You're the commander!
You can't just sit here and cry like a baby!"

At first I get mad at him.
But then, I get mad at the yelling.

I get so mad
that I tell my
crew, "Stay right
here."

And I rush out of the
Quiet Ship and race toward
the control station.
Right outside, I try to
decide if I should run back...
But I open the door.
And they both turn and look at me.
And everything gets silent.

Everything except for all the
sad inside of me so I yell,

"STOPPP YELLLLING!!!!!"

And they say absolutely nothing.
Nothing.
Nothing.

So I slam the
door behind me
and race to the ship.

I tell my crew what I did,
and they cheer so loud!
"You fixed the ship!"

I say, "TIME FOR THE COUNTDOWN!"

We scream, "5, 4, 3, 2, 1..."

But before I shout blast off,
I hear, "Quinn, what are you doing
under there?"
I want to say, "Going away on my
Quiet Ship."

But I say, "I'm scared."

Their eyes get teary,
and they speak in nice voices.
So when they open their arms,
I rush to them,
and we hug so tight.

And for the rest of that night,
all the sounds I hear
are nice
and soft
and quiet.

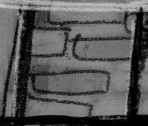

To Jade, Sage, and anyone who
needs a Quiet Ship—HA

To my family—SS

Library of Congress Cataloging-in-Publication data is on file with the publisher.

Text copyright © 2018 by Hallee Adelman
Pictures copyright © 2018 by Sonia Sánchez
First published in the United States of America in 2018 by Albert Whitman & Company
ISBN 978-0-8075-6713-5

Printed in China
10 9 8 7 6 5 4 3 2 1 HH 22 21 20 19 18

Design by Nina Simoneaux

For more information about Albert Whitman & Company,
visit our website at www.albertwhitman.com.